Lee C. Corbett

Vegetables

Lee C. Corbett

Vegetables

ISBN/EAN: 9783337369903

Printed in Europe, USA, Canada, Australia, Japan

Cover: Foto ©Andreas Hilbeck / pixelio.de

More available books at **www.hansebooks.com**

VOLUME IV. *NUMBER 14.*

BULLETIN 49.

WEST VIRGINIA

AGRICULTURAL EXPERIMENT STATION

Morgantown, W. Va.

Vegetables.

L. C. CORBETT.

MARCH, 1897.

FAIRMONT;
INDEX STEAM PRINTING HOUSE.
1897

BOARD OF REGENTS OF THE WEST VIRGINIA UNIVERSITY.

CONTENTS—BULLETIN 49.

By L. C. CORBETT.

SUMMARY.

1. The same quantity of beans planted in drills will give almost if not quite double the product they will planted in hills.

2. The yield of Lima Beans can be increased by planting the seed in inverted sods in a hotbed from April 1–10. Where but

a few plants are grown for family use, the increase will more than repay the trouble.

3. Bush Lima Beans yield well and can, I believe, be made to take the place of the pole sorts. If this is true, the cost of poles and training can be deducted from the cost of growing Lima beans.

4. The bush sorts of beans require less space for development than the pole varities, and consequently a larger return per acre may be expected from Bush Limas than from Pole Limas, particularly towards the northern limit of the successful cultivation of the Pole Limas.

5. It is believed that the limit of the successful cultivation of the Bush Lima will be found to be much farther north than that of the Pole Lima. ·

6. The test of the year shows a decided advantage in planting Peas three inches deep, as against either deeper or shallower planting.

7. The Tomatoes introduced in 1896 emphasize the great variability which this plant has acquired since it was brought under cultivation.

8. The fertilizer test on Tomatoes indicates the value of a complete manure for this crop.

9. The fertilizer test clearly shows the superiority of potasic fertilizers among the special manures used and the advantage to be gained in the use of sulphate of potash over the muriate in feitilization of Tomatoes.

10. The balance of evidence given in the test of Seedlings vs. Cuttings of Tomato plants in outdoor culture favors the cuttings both in earliness and the total crop for the season. The fruits, however, are smaller than those of the seedling plants.

11. The one test of Seedlings vs. Cuttings in the house gives a verdict decidedly in favor of the seedling plants.

12. The more care given young Tomato plants, previous to planting in the garden, the larger the yield.

13. Treating young Tomato plants, according to the best approved methods, before planting in the field, increases the yield

sufficiently to more than pay the cost of the extra equipment and labor.

14. Training Tomato plants to a single stem hastens maturity of the fruits and somewhat increases their size.

15. Tomato plants trained in racks gave a larger yield than those trained by any other method,

16. The date of seed sowing that gave the largest yield of fruit was March 2.

17. The use of a straw mulch under Tomato plants reduced the rot nearly one-half.

18. Pruning Tomato plants after the crop was set hastened the maturity of the fruits, but slightly decreased the season's crop.

VEGETABLES.

Vegetables furnish the variety for the table of both working man and millionaire. They form not only the side dishes but the main reliance in the bill of fare of nearly every household in this broad land. In some communities this is carried so far that all meat is excluded from the diet. Such people call themselves vegetarians; undoubtedly, the remote ancestors of the race belonged to this class. For, deprive man of the modern weapons and means of entraping and killing game and his meat would be meager indeed. Eggs and the young birds and animals that could not escape by their own efforts would naturally constitute the meat diet of the primitive man. Vegetables of numerous kinds were more or less abundant, and as they could be eaten without cooking they undoubtedly formed a large percentage of the daily food of these simple people. Notwithstanding the great antiquity of the vegetable diet and of some of the vegetables we to-day use, they now hold a higher rank among human food materials than ever before in the history of the race. Whole armies of workmen are annually employed, in the United States alone, in the production of this class of food. This intensive condition is rendered necessary by the demands of the present day for *fresh* products from the garden and again by the perishable nature of the commodity. This latter reason also explains why market gardening interests gather about centres of population. Consumers demand fresh products and he who comes nearest complying with this demand finds readiest sale for his merchandise.

Our State boasts few large cities, but each year chronicles in-

creasing population, both in town and village. Manufacturing
is the pursuit of a large share of this increase, and it is these
persons who patronize the huckster's wagon most liberally.
The farmer who moved to town to spend the remainder of his
days rides out to the farm for his sweet corn, tomatoes and po-
tatoes, but the man who spends eight or ten hours at the desk
or bench purchases his vegetables from the local market gardener. As I have stated, this demand is constantly increas-
ing and the young men into whose hands the lands of this State
are passing should avail themselves of the opportunities open-
ing before them.

Just now old lines of agriculture are giving place to new
ones. The products that came from these West Virginia hills a
quarter-century ago must be quite different from those that
will be produced a decade hence.

Maryland has for a number of years held the palm over all
competitors in the canning of tomatoes. Why should this be?
The Ohio River Valley and the Glade region of our State present two sections unparalleled in natural advantages for the
production of truck crops.

These are some of the reasons why the Experiment Station
annually devotes much time and energy to the testing of various methods of growing garden vegetables, for we believe that
we should encourage new industries as well as foster those that
are well established.

In considering the results recorded in this bulletin, the
reader should keep constantly before him the character of the
past season. There is no one factor entering into the growth of
plants that plays a greater part than the presence or absence
of abundant moisture. The equal of the season of 1896 has
never before been recorded. In some respects the abundance
of moisture was a benefit, while in others it was a positive in-
jury.

BEANS.

In this consideration the Bean is spoken both as a market,
garden and farm crop. In the first place a comparison of a few

varieties sent to us by various seedsmen is recorded. These were all grown from seed planted in the open. Five beans were planted in each hill, and ten hills were used in each test, so that we have in every case a comparison of the product of fifty beans. The crop is recorded in weight of snap or string beans, this being the form of product of greatest interest to the market gardener.

BUSH BEANS.

		When planted.	Harvest began.	Total yield snap beans	Yield per hill.	Yield per plant.
				lbs	lbs.	lbs.
New Stringless Green Pod	Burpee	May 7	J'ne 30	20.7	2.07	.647
Golden Wax	Rawson	"	"	22.0	2.2	.458
Kenney's Rustless G. Wax	Burpee	"	July 3	20.0	2.0	.555
Prolifie Tree..	Livingstone	"	" 7	21.5	2.15	.615
New Dwf. Wax, No. 40	Burpee	"	" 7	12.2	1.74	871
Rawson's Hort. Wax	Rawson	"	J'ne 30	19.7	2.19	.520

BEANS.—Cultural Methods.

FIELD BEANS.

It is somewhat of a surprise to note the limited extent to which this standard crop is cultivated in our State. As a rule it is more remunerative than any of the cereal grains, and has another advantage of being a splendid preparatory crop, as, in fact, are all hoe crops.

As a rule beans are planted in hills somewhat closer than corn, but so that cultivation can be carried on in both directions. This system is economical of labor, but expensive as regards the yield.

During 1895. a test of hill and drill planting was carried out, by the author, upon the prairies of the northwest. The details were as follows.*

* See South Dakota Bulletin, No. 47.

HILLS VS. DRILLS.

No.	Treatment.	Quantity of Seed.	Yield. Lbs.	Yield. Ozs.
326	Hills, 5 seed in a hill.............	500	5	15
227	Drills, 1 seed in a place, 4 ins. apart.	500	6	15
328	Hills, planted with corn-planter...	2 lbs.	12	10
329	Drill, garden drill...............	2 lbs.	31	3

"HILLS VS. DRILLS."

If we are to grow beans, what is the best and cheapest method of planting and caring for them ?

To aid prospective planters, the following simple comparisons were made · Two lots of 500 beans each of the Prolific Tree Field Bean were counted out. One set was planted in hills 18 inches apart in the row, 3 feet between rows and five beans in a place. The other set was dropped one bean in a place and 4 inches apart, in rows same distance apart as in previous case. As shown in the table, the drilled beans gave one pound more seed at harvest time than the 500 planted in hills.

To give the test more of a commercial bearing and yet keep it within bounds, two lots of two pounds each of the above named variety of beans were carefully weighed out, and one lot planted in the hills about 18 inches apart, with a hand corn-planter; the other lot of two pounds was placed in a New Model garden drill and drilled in probably 1½ inches deep.

The results of this latter case are also recorded in the table, and from the marked difference in favor of the drilled beans, I feel justified in recommending the use of the ordinary grain drill with the feed so stopped as to sow the seed in drills at the desired distance for the commercial planting of beans.

The same experiment has been repeated upon the trial grounds here this season with the same general conclusions.

The accompanying table compiled from the season's work serves to emphasize the results recorded in the above quoted experiment :

Treatment.	Quantity of Seed.	Yield. Lbs.
Hills, 18 in. in row..........................	500	18.5
Drills, beans 6 in. apart in row...............	500	33.2
Hills, 18 in apart, corn-planters..............	2 lbs.	50.7
Drills, garden seed drill	2 lbs.	140.4

A comparison of these tables shows not only the same general law, but at the same time indicates the relative yield of the same quantities of seed of the same variety in the two States.

LIMA BEANS.

There are few gardens thought to be complete unless they contain Lima beans, and besides being a constant member of the home garden, they are grown to a considerable extent by market gardeners and canners.

Like the tomato the Lima bean requires a season much longer than ours for full maturity. Whatever, even then, tends to hasten fruitfulness or to lengthen the season for this plant is of advantage. With the above object in view, several plantings of Lima beans were made at various times in the greenhouse on inverted sods.

The first planting was made March 27; a second, April 3, and a third, in doors, on April 10. On May 7 a similar planting was made in the open. The accompanying table which details the total yield from each lot for the season, also serves to indicate the relative yield to be derived by the different treatments. This also indicates the relative earliness of the several sorts.

Name	Treatment.	Date of plant-ing.	Yield of beans in pod.	Yield of shelled beans.
			lbs.	lbs.
Large White Lima...............	Sods.	Mar 27	16.6	9.
Large White Lima...............	"	Apr. 3	17.7	11.1
Large White Lima	"	" 10	17.0	10.7
Large White Lima...............	open.	May 7	8.0	4.7

The above records shows that the March planting is a little too early for best results, yet it is much more satisfactory than the out-door planting. The date giving the greatest yield was April 3, while the second best was April 10. From this it is evident that the season's crop of Lima beans can be at least doubled, while the labor of growing them on sods and transplanting to the field is no more than with cucumbers. One month's time added to the life of the Lima bean seems capable of doubling its yield. For the home garden a few hills can be grown in this way by using the space in the hotbed from which the young tomatoes were transplanted at first handling.

BUSH LIMA BEANS.

The bush Lima marks a new epoch in the culture of Lima beans. The cumbersome poles necessary for the heavy climbing vines can be abandoned, and that means no small saving both in time and money. The plants can be planted more closely than the pole varieties, hence there is a saving of land. The cultivation can be carried on by horse power more successfully than with pole beans, therefore there is a saving of labor, and while the yield per plant may not be as great, the aggregate yield per acre will, 1 am convinced, be quite as large if not greater with the dwarf sorts than with the pole beans.

At the present time we have four distinct types of the so-called dwarf Lima bean   The typical fruits of these are represented in the accompanying cut.

1. Burpee's Bush Lima

2. Henderson's Bush Lima.

3. Dreer's Thorburn's Kumerlee Dwarf Lima.

4. Jackson Dwarf Lima.

COMPARISON OF SORTS.

Name.	When planted.	Yield, pod and all.	Yield of shelled beans.	Yield per hill.
		lbs.	lbs.	lbs.
Burpee's Bush Lima	May 7	3.8	2.3	.23
Dreer's Bush Lima...	May 7	2.7	1.7	.17
Henderson's Bush Lima..........	May 7	1.6	1.0	.10
Thorburn's Bush Lima.,.........	May 7	2.5	1.9	.19

The above comparison is based on the product of 10 hills, five beans being planted in each hill. The yield is small when reckoned for each hill, but if placed upon the basis of hills 3x3 feet for an acre, the total becomes large. On this basis the Burpee Bush Lima would have produced about 12 bu. per acre which is not a low yield for field beans planted at that distance.

PEAS.

Under this title a great variety of plants might be classified, some grown for their flowers only, others for their foliage, and still others for their fruits. It is with those grown for their fruits or seeds that we are at present interested. Of this group of the pea family, we have three general classes, viz., those with hard smooth seeds of which early Kent may be taken as a type. 2. Those havi g a convoluted or wrinkled seed usually of a green color when mature 3. Those producing an edible pod which is more fleshy than that of either of the above mentioned types.

In our present study only the wrinkled class comes under consideration. These were chosen because they better represent the culinary standard of the present, and secondly because they are considered to be less hardy and vigorous than other sorts. It was thought that if deep planting was not injurious to this class, it certainly would not be to the hardier and more virile sorts belonging to the hard smooth-seeded types.

The results of the test are recorded in the appended table.

Depth of Planting.	First plants appeared.	Fully up.	Percentage matured.	Harvest began.	Weight of peas in pod.	Weight of vines.
					lbs.	lbs.
2 inches......	May 11	May 15	.87	July 13	7.9	13.4
3 inches......	May 11	May 15	.98	July 11	8.2	17 5
4 inches.....	May 12	May 15	.79	July 11	6.9	14.5
6 inches......	May 15	May 16	.68	July 11	6.5	16.3
8 inches......	May	May 19	.40	July 13	6.0	9.9

This experiment indicates a decided advantage for the seeds planted 3 inches deep. Those planted more deeply as well as those planted two inches deep, gave a lower percentage of germination, also a lessened yield. The date of edible maturity is not materially changed by the depth of planting, although those from thr e to six inches gave earlier harvest than those planted either shallower or deeper.

TOMATOES

There are few garden vegetables that lend themselves to the general farm conditions. The tomato, perhaps, more than any other vegetables belonging to the garden fulfills the requirements of a farm crop. It is not fastidious in regard to soil as is the *onion;* it requires only the cultivation demanded by corn ; it returns a product that can be harvested and marketed as easily as peaches, and is exempt from the uncertainties of late spring frosts.

While tomatoes cannot be stored and held as apples and winter pears, yet a slight approach can be made even along this line, and if canning factories are conveniently located there need be no trouble in disposing of the product of several acres at remunerative prices. Tomatoes are now-a-days so generally grown that it seems almost needless to spend time testing varieties and methods of culture. This plant, while generally classed among annual plants, is only an annual by force of circumstances. Everyone knows tha. the plant does not come to maturity, but that its career is ended each year by the advent of frost. In climates exempt from frost, as in portions of southern California, the tomato grows years after year, living sometimes to be five or six years of age. It is this indeterminate nature of the plant which makes it difficult to grow and ripen its fruit in the shor' seasons of the northwest. In this region we are not handicapped by so short a season, and as a result a larger yield per plant can be expected here than in the more northern latitudes. Because of the peculiarly fortunate placing of West Virginia as regards latitude and climate, growers should avail themselves of the natural advantages which give them a decided vantage ground in competition.

TOMATO FERTILIZER TEST.

Numerous fertilizer tests have been made with tomatoes upon soils of various natures, and it has come to be almost au axiom that tomatoes are not benefitted by nitrogenous fertilizers, while those containing large quantities of potash and phosphoric acid are most desirable. The question in mind, when the experiments here recorded were undertaken, was: Is a a complete or nearly complete fertilizer better than a special manure? If a special potash manure is desirable, is there any difference in favor of either muriate or sulphate of potash?

In order to arrive at some results that would be an index to future work along this line the various quantities and combinations of ingredients in the accompanying table were carefully weighed out.

After the plants were set, each mixture in the quantity and combination indicated was given to each plant of each particular test. In all cases *ten* plants were used, they were rown from and planted March 14, and subsequently all received like treatment except as regards the fertilizer applied. The soil used was a clay knoll upon which tomatoes had never before been grown, the land was of fair quality and had received no previous fertilizing.

FERTILIZER TEST.

TREATMENT.	Date of first ripe fruit.	No. of plants.	Avg. No. of ripe fruits per plant.	Avg. Wt. of fruits per plant, in oz.	Avg. Wt. of individual ripe fruits.	Avg. No. of ripe fruits per plant up to Sept. 1st.
Sulphate of potash, 2 oz.	July 17	10	12.6	2.8	3.6	10.6
Bone meal, 2 oz.	" 25	10	14.4	3.6	4.0	11.3
Muriate potash, 2 oz.	" 25	10	7.4	1.7	3.7	6.6
Nitrate of Soda, 2 oz.	" 17	10	7.3	1.5	3.0	6.9
Sulphate of potash, 4 oz.	" 25	10	13.8	3.5	4.0	9.6
Bone Meal, 4 oz.	" 17	10	19.7	5.3	4.0	13.1
Muriate of potash, 4 oz.	" 17	10	9.1	2.1	3.1	7.5
Nitrate of soda, 4 oz	" 31	10	7.9	1.7	3.0	7.0
* { Nitrate of soda, 1 oz Muriate of potash, 1 oz Sulphate of potash, 1 oz Bone Meal, 1 oz	July 17	10	21.8	5.4	3.9	17.3
* { Nitrate of soda, 2 oz Sulphate of potash, 2 oz	July 25	10	10.8	2.2	3.0	9.4
* { Nitrate of soda, 2 oz Muriate of potash, 2 oz	July 25	10	8.0	1.8	3.1	7.1
* { Nitrate of soda, 2 oz Muriate of potash, 4 oz	July 17	10	15.5	3.6	3.1	12.3
* { Nitrate of soda, 2 oz Sulphate of potash, 4 oz	July 25	10	25.2	6.7	4.0	16.2
* { S lphate of potash, 4 oz Bone Meal, 2 oz	July 31	10	18.9	5.8	4.1	13.1
* { Muriate of potash, 1 oz Bone Meal, 2 oz	July 17	10	20.2	5.1	4.0	14.1
No fertilizer used.	" 31	10	9.0	2.5	4.9	8.5

* Mixture.

The results are very pronounced both in the yield of fruits
per plant as well as in the size of the individual fruits. It is
evident that we can not afford to apply nitrate of soda as a
special manure to tomatoes. The use of this special fertilizer
gave not only the smallest but also the fewest fruits per plant.
Fine ground bone meal gave the best return of any of the
special manures used, while sulphate of potash is a good second. There is quite as marked a difference in the results obtained from muriate of potash, sulphate of potash as there
is between any other two combinations of fertilizers
used. This holds good for each combination into which
either muriate or sulphate of potash enters. An increase
in the quantity of sulphate of potash used, marks a corresponding increase in the fruitfulness of the vines to

which it was applied, both when used alone and in combination with nitrate of soda. It is worthy of note, however, that
the second largest yield was that received when an application
of one ounce each of muriate of potash, sulphate of potash, nitrate of soda and bone meal were used. This made a more
nearly complete fertilizer than any other single combination
used. In all cases, except where nitrate of soda was used, the
application of fertilizer gave a remunerative increase in yield
over the check plants or those upon which no fertilizer was
used.

PRUNING TO HASTEN MATURITY.

Many growers of tomatoes, after the desired quantity of fruit
has set, cut off the new shoots that appear upon their plants.
This operation is akin to that of pruning fruit trees to reduce
the number of fruits carried. In the case of the tomato, however, the pruning is done for the purpose of hastening maturity
of the fruits regardless of their size. The results of the season
indicate that the general practice is well founded, but that the
size of the fruits is not necessarially increased by the operation
as is the case when fruit trees are pruned or the fruit is thinned.

PRUNING TO HASTEN MATURITY.

Garden No.	TREATMENT.	No. of plants.	Date of bloom.	Date of first ripe fruits.	Avg. No. ripe fruits per plant.	Avg. Wt. of fruits per plant in pounds.	Avg. Wt. of individual ripe fruits in ounces.	Avg. No. of ripe fruits per plant up to Sept. 1st.
14-16	Plants pruned after fruit set...	10	June 1	July 17	37.2	8.4	3.6	36.6
14-17	Check for 14-16, not pruned.....	10	June 1	July 17	38.6	10.4	4.3	35.3

The pruned plants gave a larger number of ripe fruits per
plant up to Sept. 1 than those not pruned. The total yield per
plant is less than in the normal plants and the fruits were
smaller.

TIME OF SEED SOWING.

Some maintain that as good or better crops of tomatoes can be grown from seeds planted in the open after the ground has become sufficiently warm to cause germination as can be produced from hotbed grown transplanted plants. It is not the purport of the present test to settle this point, but on the contrary to determine if possible the advantage of any particular date between Feb 10 and April 10 for seed sowing.

Seeds of Dwarf Champion Tomatoes were sown at intervals of ten days from Feb. 10 to April 10, making seven plantings upon the dates indicated in the accompanying table.

TIME OF SEED SOWING.

Garden No.	NAME.	Date of seed sowing.	Date of first ripe fruits.	No. of plants.	Avg. No. of ripe fruits per plant.	Avg. Wt. of fruits per plant in oz.	Avg. Wt. of individual ripe fruits.	Avg. No. of ripe fruits per plant up to Sept. 1st.
13	Dwarf Champion	Feb. 10	July 17	10	28.5	5.6	3.0	25.9
"	" "	" 20	" 21	10	20.5	3.9	3.0	20.1
"	" "	Mar. 2	" 21	10	30.9	6 9	3.1	24.9
"	" "	" 10	" 21	10	15.7	3.3	3.0	14.4
"	" "	" 20	" 17	10	28.5	6.3	3.1	24.3
"	" "	" 30	" 25	10	15.8	3.5	3.1	14.0
"	" "	April 9	" 21	10	20.5	4.5	3.1	17.9

The results detailed in the table indicate that the largest crop can be expected from plants grown from seeds sown on or about the first of March. The fruits from this batch of plants were both larger and more abundant than those from any other date.

METHODS OF HANDLING PLANTS.

To persons not experienced in raising tomatoes, the growing of the young plants is a great barrier because of the equipment and care necessary. The cost of plants at ordinary prices to set an acre would be enough to deter many from entering the business, The space necessary for the seed bed is small compared with that necessary to accommodate the plants for the last two weeks before they are set in the field, provided they are given pots or tomato-cans as described in Bulletin 42 of this Station. Any one can afford a hotbed sufficient size to start the seedling plants, but the question of cold-frames or greenhouse large enough to protect the plants before they go to the field, is another question. This test was instituted to determine the question of the advisibility of transplanting the plants directly from the hotbed to the field without previous handling. Then too, such plants can be set with a dibble much more rapidly than those grown in pots. Pot grown plants must have holes dug for them and this in connection with the additional time required in setting adds considerably to the cost of the crop.

In all cases, plants of Livingston's Beauty, grown from the same seed sowing, were used in these tests, the only difference in the history of the several lots being in the manner of treating them between the time of vegetation and the date of planting them in the field.

The set marked 14-8 were not removed from the seedbed until they were transplanted to the garden. They were densely crowded together and were what the gardeners term leggy plants. In addition to this, they were, in order to reduce expenses, set in the field with a dibble. The lot numbered 14-9 were treated in like manner except that they were removed from the hotbed with more care and were set in holes which had previously been dug for them. No. 14-10 were transplanted from the seedbed to flats on April 3 and again April 20, and when set in the field, May 13, holes were prepared for them. Lot No. 14-11 were transplanted on April 3 to flats, and on April 20 they were placed in 1-qt. vegetable cans. When set in the field on the same day as the other plants of the test, holes were dug for them. Lot No. 14-12 were transplanted to 2-in. pots on April 3 and to 3½-in. pots on April 20 and set in holes when transferred to the field on May 13. The last set No. 14-13 were transplanted into a flat April 3 and were transferred to another flat, allowing them more room, on April 20. When taken to the field the dirt was shaken from the roots and the plants set with a dibble the same as lot 14-8.

The treatment given the several sets of plants varies from the least expensive and most careless, to the most careful approved manner of pot growing.

METHOD OF HANDLING PLANTS.

Garden No.	TREATMENT.	No. of plants.	Date of bloom.	Date of first ripe fruits.	Avg. No. ripe fruits per plant.	Avg. Wt. of fruits per plant in lbs.	Avg. Wt. of individual ripe fruits in oz.	Avg. No. of ripe fruits per plant up to Sept. 1st.	Yield per acre in bu.
14-8	From hotbed, not previously transplanted, set with dibble	10	June 1	July 28	38.5	9.9	4.0	33.7	449.1
14-9	Plants same as 14-8 set in holes	10	June 6	July 28	40.4	11.8	4.7	35.2	535.3
14-10	Plants from hotbed to flats, to field in holes	10	June 1	July 17	41.6	11.3	4.4	38.2	512.6
14-11	Plants from hotbed to cans, to field in holes	10	June 1	July 17	45.5	12.6	4.4	41.8	571.6
14-12	Plants from hotbed to pots, to field in holes	10	June 9	July 21	55.5	15.3	4.4	50.9	694.1
14-13	Plants from hotbed to flats, to field with dibble	10	June 1	July 17	40.2	11.5	4.6	38.3	521.7

From this record it is obvious that the best treatment gives the largest returns both for the total yield of the season and up to September 1st. This manner of treating plants is superior to any other method used. The use of the vegetable can as a substitute for the pot, being the next best treatment, gives results second only to those of the pot grown plants. The differences shown by the other sets of plants are less marked and none are sufficiently better than the first, or that numbered 14-8, to warrant any extra outlay. In the instance of 14-12, which is considered the best and which is the most approved method of handling tomato plants, I consider the increased yield more than enough to justify the necessary outlay in the construction of cold frames and purchase of pots for the market gardener or commercial grower.

STRAW MULCH VS. ROT.

In Bulletin 42 a preliminary test of the use of the straw mulch as a preventative measure for tomato rot was favorably reported. The results of the present season enforce the conclusions there drawn, but because of the unprecedented rainfall of the year the use of the fungicides was of no avail and this feature of the test was abandoned. The accompanying record of the mulched and check set, the plants which were allowed to grow at will upon the ground, speaks more emphatically in favor of the use of the mulch than did the work of last season, although the percentage of rot on both sets was much less this year.

STRAW MULCH VS. ROT.

Garden No.	TREATMENT.	No. of plants.	Date of bloom.	Date of first ripe fruits.	Avg. No. ripe fruits per plant.	Avg. Wt. of fruits per plant in lbs.	Avg. Wt. of individual fruits in oz.	Avg. No. of ripe fruits per plant up to Sept. 1st.	Percentage of rot.
14-14	Mulched with straw, June 19...	10	June 1	July 17	53.6	14.6	4.4	48.8	(*)
14-15	Check for 14-14	10	June 1	July 17	46.2	12.2	4.3	41.5	(†)

* .0097 or .97 of 1 per cent.   † .0188 or 1.88 per cent.

TOMATO TRAINING.

Garden No.	VARIETY.	Date of first ripe fruits.	No. of plants.	Avg. No. ripe fruits per plant.	Avg. Wt. of fruits per plant in oz.	Avg. Wt. of individual ripe fruits.	Avg. No. of ripe fruits per plant up to Sept. 1st.	Treatment.
14	Beauty	July 21	10	57.6	16.5	1.6	53.1	Rack.
14	Beauty	July 17	10	15.7	5.4	5.5	15.1	Single Stem.
14	Beauty	July 17	10	41.2	11.2	4.3	40.	Inclined Lathe.
14	Beauty	July 17	10	40.4	11.1	1.4	36.6	Crossleg Support.
14	Beauty	July 21	10	43.9	11.7	4.5	42.2	Wire Trellis.
14	Beauty	July 17	10	39.4	10.1	1.1	37.7	Wire Netting.
14	Beauty	July 17	10	33.8	9.1	4.3	33.2	Check.

In some localities the commercial growing of tomatoes is dis
couraged by the belief that in order to get merchantable crops
of ripe fruits the vines must be trained in some way. Repeated
tests have been made at the several Experiment Stations
throughout the country which conclusively disprove this belief,
yet, knowing that these results are not available and not generally known, I have, during the season, repeated the experiments recorded in Bulletin 47 of the S. D. Station pages 16 and
17. The same general law holds in both cases. Single stem
training gives somewhat earlier and larger fruits but very considerably lessens the total crop. Racks in the last case gave a
somewhat larger yield of fruits per plant and the fruits averaged larger than those of any other style of training except the
single stem. Other styles of trellis used do not give enough
increase in yield over plants not trained to warrant the trouble
and expense of building them.

SEEDLINGS VS. CUTTINGS.

Since 1891 the writer has each year grown seedling and cutting plants of tomatoes for the purpose of arriving at some con-
clusion in regard to the relative time at which cuttings should
be made from which to grow plants to compare justly with
seedling plants of the same variety. The results of the various
tests have themselves been somewhat variable, but the balance

of the evidence all tends in one direction, i. e., that cutting plants are earlier than seedling but correspondingly less productive except in a few cases. A second question in the study is, do plants degenerate in vitality because of being grown from cuttings? This division of the subject is by no means yet completed. Several successive generations of cuttings from cuttings have been made and the stock is at present in the greenhouse awaiting the coming season for outdoor planting.

The history of the work is as follows:
Cornell Bulletin No. 45.

Seedlings vs. Cuttings. In 1890, seedling tomato plants gave twice as heavy yields as cuttings of equal age. In 1891, seedlings gave earlier fruits, and with one variety—Lorillard—the yield was also much greater from cuttings, while in the Ithaca it was less. Secondary cuttings, that is, cuttings taken from the cutting plants, gave much larger yields than their parents, but the crop was much later. These experiments were repeated this year (1892). The stock from which all the lots of this year came was one fine seedling plant of unknown parentage, of the peach type, which came up in our forcing-houses. Late in winter, strong cuttings were taken from the axillary shoots of this plant and were set out regularly in our tomato house. In March, therefore, we had the one old or parent plant, still in full vigor, which we shall call "A" and a small brood of cutting plants which we shall call, collectively, "B."

March 29, 12 cuttings were taken from "A." * * * At the same time seeds were sown from fruits on the same plant. The two lots were thereafter treated as nearly alike as possible. They were set side by side in the field June 1. Their behavior was as follows:

SEEDLINGS VS CUTTINGS (to frost).

Sample (March 29).	First picking.	Avg. No. fruits per plant.	Avg. Wt.of fruits per plant.	Avg. Wt. of ind. fruits.
Seedlings...............	Aug 22	23.6	3 0 lbs	2.0 oz
Cuttings...............	Aug. 3	4 30	4.8 lbs	1.8 oz

Here, then, the cuttings were much earlier and more productive than the seedlings. May 3, another batch of cuttings was taken from the old plant A. Seedlings were started from the same plant at the same time, and the two lots were placed in the field side by side. The results are like those above, only less pronounced:

SEEDLINGS VS. CUTTINGS (to frost).

Sample (May 3).	First picking.	Av. No. fruits per plant.	Av. Wt of fruits per plant.	Av. Wt of ind. fruits.
Seedlings............	Sept. 2	12	2.1 lbs.	2.9 oz.
Cuttings.............	Aug. 22	15 3	2.3 lbs.	2.3 oz.

In South Dakota Bulletin No. 37, I recorded the following experience with cutting and seedling plants:

The tomato is easily propagated by cuttings and some growers claim that cutting plants are enough superior to seedlings to justify the trouble and expense of keeping over a few plants to take cuttings from for the early crop. If cutting plants are

TABLE VI.—SEEDLINGS VS. CUTTINGS. 491

enough superior to justify this trouble in other localities, it is worthy of consideration here where the fruiting season is short.

An experiment along this line was undertaken, and the cutting plants were compared with seedlings of the same variety, and with the parent plant itself. Instead, however, of using plants that had been kept over, hot house grown plants of the variety "Earliest of All," from seed, planted January 16, were used. On April 18 following, cuttings were made from the leaders of some thirty good vigorous specimens and planted in the propagating bench of the greenhouse. The bench is heated by hot water pipes which are arranged beneath it, and is maintained at a temperature of about 68° F. The bed is composed of about three and one half inches of coarse lake sand, underlaid with about one and one half inches of clinkers. No covering sash were used, so the air about the cuttings was not close. Under these conditions the slips were sufficiently rooted in fourteen days to be transplanted to individual pots. The seedling plants used in the test were from the same seed sowing, and were grown under the same conditions as those from which the cuttings were taken. The plants, from which the cuttings were taken, were retained and set in the field for comparison. The accompanying table records the yield of ripe fruits upon each plat of twenty plants, up to and including Aug. 28.

TABLE VI.—SEEDLINGS VS. CUTTINGS.

Variety— "Earliest of All."	No. fruits till frost.	Wt. of fruit to frost. lbs.	oz.	Av. Wt. of fruit per plant.	Av. No. fruits per plants.	Av. Wt. individual fruits.
Normal	293	38	1	1.9	14.65	2.09
Parent............	287	36	4	1.81	14.35	2.00
Cuttings	479	57	13	2.87	24.00	1.90

From this it will be noted that the cutting plants gave much the greater yield, both in number of fruits and in total weight, although the fruits themselves were smaller than those of either the normal or the parent plants. This shows that the cutting plants were decidedly earlier than the seedlings, and at the same time more productive, a fact that could hardly have been hoped for.*

Table VII gives a further record of these plants carrying them to the close of the season, but recording only the ripe fruits.

TABLE VII.—SEEDLINGS VS. CUTTINGS.

Variety— "Earliest of All."	No. fruits for season.	Total Wt. of fruit for season.		Av. Wt. of fruits per plants.	Av. No. fruits per plant.	Av. Wt. of individual fruits.
		lbs.	oz.			
Normal	993	98		4.9	49.65	1.57
Parent.............	1533	146	14	7.3	76.65	1.53
Cuttings	1432	128	13	6.37	71.6	1.43

A study of this table shows that the cuttings were surpassed by those from which they were originally taken, but they maintained their lead over the seedling plants throughout the season.

From S. D. Bulletin 47, I take the record of another year, which is in the main quite contradictory to the experience above recorded.

SEEDLINGS VS. CUTTINGS.

For an early fruit crop the value of cuttings was formerly advocated as oppose 1 to plants grown from seed sown but a short period before the plants are to be set in the field.

Obviously if there are any advantages to be gained by the

* See Cornell University Bulletin 21, 1890; 32, 1891; 45, 1892.

use of such plants over seedling plants there are likewise hindrances equally as great. The difficulty of carrying through the winter plants from which to make the necessary cuttings is a serious and, in most cases, an insurmountable obstacle to the ordinary grower, while the seeds can be had at small cost and are easily stored.

Notwithstanding the adverse and discouraging aspect of the problem a series of tests were instituted. The original stock of cuttings was taken from a plant grown from the same general seed sowing as the other plants used in the trials during the season of 1894. As noted, the cuttings were made October 5, and their subsequent history is detailed in the table.

SEEDLINGS VS. CUTTINGS

No.	TREATMENT.	No. plants.	Date of bloom.	First ripe fruits.	No. fruits per plant.	Weight of fruits per plant in pounds.	Weight of individual fruits in ounces.	No. fruits to Aug. 31.	Weight of fruits per plant to Aug. 31 in ozs.
165	Early Ruby, (seedlings)	50	June 17	Aug. 6	32.6	6.47	3.17	4.40	12.22
166	Early Ruby, (cuttings), made Oct. 5th, 1894	1-2	June 28	Aug. 30	9.57	2.90	3.75	.14	.57
168	Early Ruby, (c'ttings), made Dec. 19, 1894	10	Jun. 18	Aug. 13	22.5	3.40	3.44	4.00	7.87
169	Early Ruby, (cuttings), from 167, made March 11, 1895	2-7	June 18	July 26	10.5	3.36	3.61	.30	.62
170	Early Ruby, (cuttings), from 168, made April 16, 1895	7	July 1	Aug. 30	30.0	3.70	2.65	2.00	6.50
171	Dwarf Champion, (seed), seed sown Jan. 16, 1895	7	June 18	Aug. 16	26.7	4.00	2.40	1.43	2.68
172	Dwarf Champion, (cuttings), from 171, made April 16, 1895	7	June 18	Aug. 9	18.2	2.82	2.42	2.14	4.28

So far as the general crop of the season is concerned, the cuttings fell far in the rear of the plants grown from seed. The only advantage possessed over the seedling plants is the fact that the cuttings from the time they are made until they are ready to go into the field occupy the space of the greenhouse a shorter period than do the seedling plants.

In the case of 171 and 172 there was a decided advantage in the earliness of the cuttings over the parent plants. Up to Aug. 31, the cuttings had yielded 1.6 oz. per plant more. This amount even upon a thousand plants would only aggregate 100 lbs., a gain too small to be taken into consideration when the additional work is taken into account. But should a person, possessing only a limited stock of some choice variety, desire to increase it and at the same time hasten the maturity of the product, the plants might be treated as were those of No. 171. The tops were cut out and rooted as cuttings and the root and stalk retained to make a second growth.

The results recorded up to this point have, in every case, come from experience with out-door grown plants.

We have now to record the results of a test of Seedling vs. Cutting Plants for House Tomatoes.

SEEDLING VS. CUTTING PLANTS FOR HOUSE TOMATOES.

During the winter of 1895 and '96, a careful test of the comparative value of cutting and seedling plants of three standard varieties of tomatoes was carried on in the forcing houses of the West Virginia Experiment Station. The varieties of plants used were Livingston's Beauty, Acme and Liberty Bell. There were two sets of cuttings made from plants which had borne a crop of fruit in the greenhouse, the parent plants grew from seeds sown on July 27, 189 . On Nov. 13, the first set of cutting were made, and the second set on Dec. 17 of the same year. On Nov. 14, 18 5, seeds were sown from which all the seedling plants used in the test grew.

The plants all had careful and similar treatment, but for some reason the second cuttings were inferior to those made in

November, and all were less vigorous than the seedlings, due, undoubtedly, to a more or less devitalized condition of the parent plants from which they were taken. Nearly all responded to the condition of the tomato house, and with the exception of one lot of Acme's, all did well and made a normal growth.

The following table gives in a brief and concise form the relative earliness and the product of the several sets of plants under consideration.

SEEDLINGS VS. CUTTINGS IN HOUSE.

KIND.	No. plants.	Seed sown or cutting made.	Date of bloom.	First ripe fruit.	No. of fruits.	Weight of fruits.	Avg. No. fruits per plant.	Wt. of fruits per plant.	Avg. Wt. of individual fruits.
						lbs.		lbs.	oz.
Liberty Bell, [light house]									
Cuttings—1st	9	Nov. 13	3-2	4-28	76	13.4	8 4-9	1.488	.176
Cuttings—2d	9	Dec. 17	3-10	5-2	86	8.3	9 5-9	.922	.096
Seedlings	20	Nov. 14	2-31	4-21	318	42.2	17.4	2.01	1.71
Acme, [light house]									
Cuttings—1st	4	Nov. 13	2-15	4-28	72	11.3	18.0	2.825	1.56
Cuttings—2d	3	Dec. 17	3-15	5-6	17	3.1	5.66	1.03	.18
Seedlings	11	Nov. 14	1-31	4-14	165	29.2	15.0	2.60	1.77
Acme, [dark house]									
Cuttings—1st	5	Nov. 13	3-3	4-23	58	9.6	11.6	1.92	1.65
Cuttings—2d	4	Dec. 17	3-23	5-12	46	6.2	11.5	1.55	1.31
Seedlings	9	Nov. 14	2-11	4-21	128	30.4	19.8	3.38	1.70
Beauty, [dark house]									
Cuttings—1st	10	Nov. 13	2-26	4-25	127	25.0	12.7	2.5	1.96
Cuttings—2d	10	Dec. 17	3-27	5-6	73	14.2	7.9	1.42	1.59
Seedlings	30	Nov. 14	2-11	4-21	366	89.4	18.3	3.47	1.88
						282.3			

As is noted in the sub-heads in the table, one half of the plants of this test were subjected to the influence of an incandescent gas light, produced from eight No. 34 Welsbach Burners. The house was divided by opaque curtains which were slid back during the day and drawn across the middle of the house during the night. As will be noted, a larger yield was received from the plants in the dark house than from those in the light. Very marked influence was shown upon the radish corresponding to that obtained at the Cornell Station from the use of the Electric Arc light. The influence of the gas light upon lettuce is not marked, but as only one series of tests have been carried on along this line, it is too early to state conclusions. The indications are, however, that we shall find that the incandescent gas light has the same influence upon vegetation as does the incandescent Arc Electric light.

Second :—The verdict of this experiment with seedling and cutting plants is that for purposes of forcing there is no advantage, but rather a loss to be derived from the use of cutting plants. There is not a single exception to this statement in the trial of nine different sets of plants as recorded in the above table.

The general crop of the whole house was more than gratifying, as the plants averaged 2.3 lbs. of fruit each, aggregating 263.3 lbs. for the house, and two crops were taken from Oct. 1, 1895, to June 1, 1896.

SEEDLINGS VS. CUTTINGS. (in garden during 1896).

This test was a continuation of the work carried on in the greenhouse during the winter of 1895-'96.

The history of the plants used is as follows :—The plants from which the cuttings used in this test came, were cuttings grown in the greenhouse—second crop of 1895-'96—and these in turn came from plants grown in the greenhouse—first crop of winter of 1895-'96—the seed from which the last named plants came was sown July 27, 1895. The history of the house grown plants, which were the parents of the set now under discussion, has been given in the preceding division.

In this case three sets of secondary cuttings, or cuttings of cuttings, were made on March 12th, 20th and 31st from the plants known as 1st cuttings. These are spoken of as:

First cuttings, 1st made March 12th.
"   "   2d   "   "   20th.
"   "   3d   "   "   31st.

From these plants, known as second cuttings, two sets of secondary, or cuttings of cuttings, were made on March 12th and 20th, respectively, except in the case of Liberty Bell from which three sets were made on the same dates as those of the first cuttings.

These plants are spoken of as:

Second cuttings, 1st made March 12th.
"   "   2d   "   "   20th.
"   "   3d   "   "   31st.

The seedling plants which were used in comparison with these cuttings came from three seed sowings, made March 18th, 20th and 31st, respectively. The idea of this seeming irregularity was to determine, if practicable, what interval should intervene between seed sowing and the making of cuttings in order that the results should be on a just basis for comparison.

The accompanying table records the results of the work of the season of 1896.

SEEDLINGS VS. CUTTING, 1896.

Garden No.	Varieties	Treatment	Date of Cutting made or Seeding.	Number of Plants.	Date of Bloom.	Date of First Ripe Fruits.	Average No. of Ripe Fruits per Plant.	Average weight of Fruits per Plant in lb.	Average weight of individual ripe Fruits in in.	Average No. of Ripe Fruits per Plant up to September 1st.
3	Acme	1st cutting, 1st made	Mar 2	5	June 9	July 13	53.6	16.4	4.8	45.0
"	"	Seedling	Mar 29	5	June 11	July 11	33.8	4.6	3.0	15.6
"	"	1st Cutting, 2d made	Mar 20	5	June 1	July 55	41.8	12.8	4.9	37.0
"	"	Seedling	Mar 31	5	June 9	July 17	53.8	4.2	2.9	21.0
"	"	1st Cutting, 3d made	Mar 22	5	June 15	July 55	54.6	12.8	3.6	40.0
"	"	Seedling	Mar 18	5	June 9	July 13	61.6	15.8	4.0	57.6
"	"	2d Cutting, 1st made		5			44.8	13.8	4.6	34.8
"	"	Seedling		5			44.8	9.2	3.0	32.4
11	Livingston Beauty	1st Cutting, 1st made	Mar 22	5	June 1	July 17	47.6	15.0	5.0	41.6
"	"	Seedling	Mar 18	5	June 15	July 55	36.4	10.4	4.5	29.2
"	"	1st Cutting, 2d made	Mar 29	5	June 2	July 28	41.8	11.6	4.0	37.0
"	"	Seedling	Mar 30	5	June 9	July 55	56.8	1.0	4.8	30.0
"	"	2d Cutting, 1st made	Mar 18	5	June 9	July 55	36.8	12.2	5.0	35.8
"	"	Seedling	Mar 30	5	June 15	July 51	56.8	17.2	4.8	42.2
"	"	2d Cutting, 2d made	Mar 30	5	June 15	July 55	38.6	12.2	5.0	31.4
"	"	Seedling	Mar 31	5	June 15	July 25	38.0	10.0	4.2	28.8
"	"	1st Cutting, 3d made	Mar 31	5	June 15	Aug 4	38.6	12.0	4.9	34.6
"	"	Seedling		5			30.8	7.8	4.0	30.8
41	Liberty Belle	1st Cutting, 1st made	Mar 12	5	June 9	July 11	76.6	19.6	4.0	54.2
"	"	Seedling	Mar 12	5	June 9	July 55	70.6	16.6	3.7	54.2
"	"	2d Cutting, 1st made	Mar 18	5	June 15	July 17	60.0	11.6	3.1	46.8
"	"	Seedling	Mar 30	5	June 1	July 28	29.0	6.0	3.3	17.2
"	"	1st Cutting, 2d made	Mar 30	5	June 15	July 13	50.4	12.6	4.0	4.8
"	"	Seedling	Mar 20	5	June 15	July 55	36.0	9.2	4.0	24.4
"	"	2d Cutting, 2d made	Mar 30	5	June 15	July 55	45.0	10.4	3.7	38.2
"	"	Seedling	Mar 31	5	June 15	July 13	34.6	7.8	3.8	30.2
"	"	1st Cutting, 3d made	Mar 31	5	June 9	Aug 6	32.9	7.6	3.4	22.8
"	"	Seedling	Mar 31	5	June 22	July 55	38.4	6.6	2.7	35.6
"	"	2d Cutting, 3d made	Mar 31	5	June 22	July 55	45.3	11.0	3.9	35.2
"	"	Seedling		5			54.6	12.2	3.6	32.8

SEEDLINGS VS. CUTTINGS, 1896.

The Acme used in this test gave earlier fruits from the cutting plants in every case, except first cuttings, third made, March 31st, in which case the date of ripening is the same as in No. 4, where the seed was sown March 20th. The total yield for the season, as well as the yield up to Sept. 1st, is greater from the cutting plants in all cases, except No. 6—seed sown March 31st. It must be borne in mind that these plants were cuttings from cuttings. Livingston's Beauty repeats the same story given by Acme, No. 6 again giving a larger yield than the cutting plants with which it was compared. The difference in this case is that No. 6 Beauty seeds were sown on March 18, instead of March 31st, as in the case of Acme and the cuttings with which it is compared were made on March 12th, instead of March 31st, as in the case with the Beauty plants. Nos. 9 and 10 of the Beauty set which correspond in date with No. 5 and 6 of the Acme set, contradict the results shown by the Acme's. Liberty Bell, practically, corroberates the evidence given by the other two tests. The cutting plants gave as early or earlier product in all cases, except in the case of No. 10, and although the date of ripening is earlier for No. 9 than for No. 10, the quantity of fruit produced up to Sept. 1st is greater and yet the yield in lbs. is most in case of No. 9.

These results conform with results obtained at Cornell in 1892 and with those at the South Dakota Station in 1893. Yet, they are contradictory to those obtained in Dakota in 1895 and also reverse the record of the parent plants grown in the forcing houses at this Station during the winter of '95 and '96. Why there should be this difference in results is a question that I am not yet prepared to answer. If we were more familiar with the problem of phenology or the influence of climate on plants, the answer to these questions might be easily solved, as it is, we can only draw general conclusions from the experience of a series of tests.

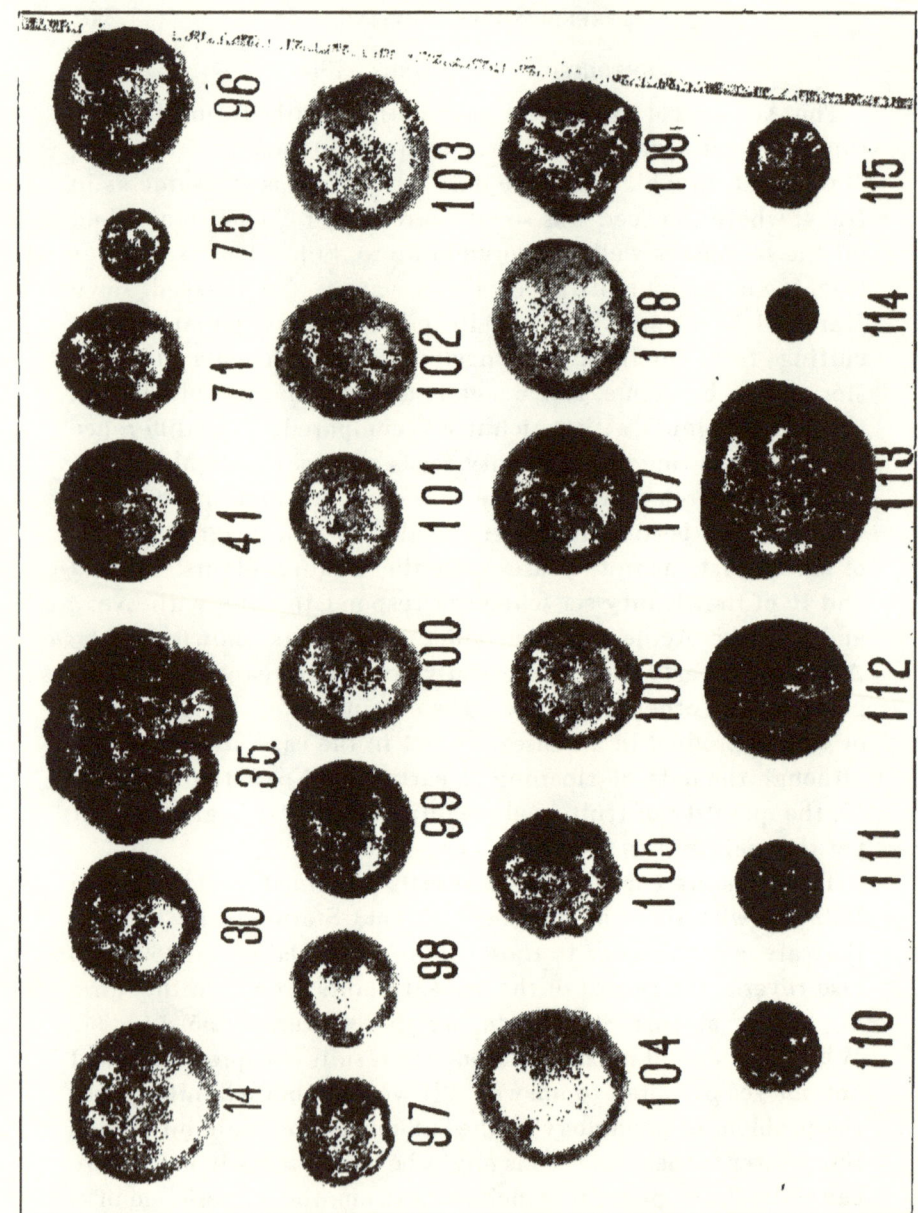

Varieties of Tomatoes Grown in 1896.

The Nos. correspond to the name Nos. used in Table, page 504.

VARIETY TEST. 1896.

Each year the catalogues contain the names of before unknown varieties or strains of tomatoes. These are placed before the public for their acceptance. It, therefore, becomes a
duty of the Experiment Station to grow these sorts and to re-
port the experience, for what it is worth, to growers as well as
introducers.

In all tests, such as here reported. which have only extended
over a single season, the conclusions should not be taken as
final, but rather as suggestive in that they point out the course
which any plant is liable to take under the conditions of soil
and climate existing in that locality during that particular
year.

We often look upon the great increase in the list of varieties
as a misfortune. This is true if the so-called additions are old
sorts with new names, but if on the other hand the novelties
represent truly new sorts possessing intrinsic worth in some
particular locality, then it should be received with favor. Tomatoes, like apples, have certain varieties which do better in
one locality than in any other. It is our business to find out
which sort is particularly adapted to the various sections of
West Virginia, and this can only be accomplished by co-opera-
tive experiments with persons in various sections of the State.
Correspondence is, therefore, solicited.

In the following table I have endeavored to indicate the comparative fruitfulness of the several varieties, the size of the
fruits as well as the earliness.

All plants were grown from seeds sown the same day. The
after treatment of the young plants was the same both before
and after setting in the garden. Every condition of the test
was made as nearly uniform as practicable for each variety so
that differences noted should be assigned to varietal variation
rather than to differences in method of treatment.

TOMATO VARIETIES COMPARED.

Garden No.	VARIETY	SEEDMAN	Date of first ripe fruits.	No. of plants.	Avg. No. ripe fruits per plant.	Avg. Wt. of fruits per plant in lbs.	Avg. Wt. of individual ripe fruits in oz.	Avg. No. ripe fruits per plant up to Sep. 1.	Percentage of rot.	Yield per acre in bu. 272.22 plants per acre.	Yield per acre in bu. up to Sep. 1.	REMARKS
14	Beauty	Livingston's Sons	July 17	10	57.9	14.9	4.1	54.9	15.9	675.9	656.9	
30	Fordhook First	Burpee	" 13	10	54.2	10.5	3.1	53.9	24.2	476.3	475.8	Stop'd fruiting Aug. 11
35	Crimson Cushion	Henderson	" 17	10	55.3	10.8	2.1	54.6	26.3	459.9	479	Stop'd fruiting Aug. 11
71	Boyd's Early Minnesota	Iowa Seed Co	" 13	10	87.8	11.2	6.1	86.6	7.1	508.1	508.1	
41	Liberty Bell	Livingston's Sons	" 17	10	61.2	12.8	3.3	55.8	18.3	536.6	528.5	
75	Vaughn's Earliest of All	Vaughn	" 3	10	65.	9.4	2.4	65.	18.5	380.	380.	
96	Pearce's Star	Pearce's Seed Store, London, Ont.	" 17	10	41.7	10.7	4.1	39.6	16.1	465.4	475.9	
97	Early Leader	Landreth	" 13	10	47.3	8.3	3.2	47.3	26.	316.5	379.2	
98	Two Celled Cross	"	" 18	10	102.5	13.6	3.	101.6	8.4	616.9	611.5	
99	Cross Bred	"	" 17	10	76.5	13.6	3.	75.3	11.9	616.9	610.6	
100	Cross Bred	"	" 13	10	82.4	14.6	2.5	81.5	10.7	662.3	656.9	
101	Three Celled Cross	"	" 17	10	102.4	16.1	3.4	102.0	6.2	730.4	731.7	
102	Large Red Olive Cross	"	" 13	10	73.6	15.8	3.8	71.1	9.1	716.7	704.5	
103	Imperial	Burpee	" 17	10	47.4	11.2	4.1	47.2	12.9	508.1	505.7	Stop'd fruiting Aug. 21
104	Waldorf	Thorburn	" 17	10	55.8	14.4	3.3	53.6	15.1	653.2	683.6	
105	Thorburn's New York	T. W. Wood & Son	" 21	10	34.7	11.7	3.3	35.8	11.6	530.7	532.6	
106	Imperial Extra Early	Johnson and Stokes	" 17	10	10.9	7.2	4.	34.3	8.4	325.6	321.1	
107	The Fortune	Maule	" 17	10	40.6	10.9	3.2	40.4	12.3	494.1	495.8	
108	New Imperial	Livingston's Sons	" 13	10	45.5	11.2	4.	45.4	15.4	508.1	509.9	
109	Early Ruby	South Dakota Station	" 17	10	65.	12.8	3.2	65.	13.4	560.6	582.5	Stop'd fruiting Aug. 14
110	Livingston's Gold Ball		" 17	10	188.4	13.5	1.2	182.1	1.2	612.4	592.9	
111			" 17	10	138.2	10.3	1.2	133.9	1.8	467.2	461.8	
112	Dakota	S. D. Station, H. C. Warner	" 17	10	36.3	9.6	4.2	35.5	14.3	435.5	434.6	
113	West Va. Seedling	S. D. Station	" 21	10	28.5	13.5	7.6	28.1	11.9	612.4	615.1	
115	Early Leader	Vick	" 13	10	34.9	5.9	2.7	34.9	15.2	267.6	271.3	Stop'd fruiting Aug. 11

The above table reveals the fact that large size in fruits is incompatible with great numbers. That the greatest yield in bushels is to be expected from plants producing fruits of medium-large size. That Nos. 35 and 113 produced the largest fruits, while 110 and 111 (which were the same variety) produced the greatest number. In earliness as is indicated by the column of yield *up to Sept. 1st*, there is no very marked difference. Nos. 75, 97, 101, 105, 108, 109 and 115 had each matured their crop at that date.

The season of 1896 presented some very peculiar freaks, one of which was the way in which the tomtoes bore and ripened their fruits. Usually the tomato continues to bloom and set fruit from the beginning of the season until the vines are killed by frost. This year fruit set as abundantly as usual, early in the season. These fruits grew to maturity and ripened, but previous to the ripening of these fruits, there had been a general failure of the bloom to set fruit, so that for a period there was no ripe fruits upon the plants, even though a part of a normal crop had previously been harvested. Some plants ceased fruiting altogether after the first effort, while others remained fruitful, and after the lapse of a few weeks again ripened fruit.

To show this peculiarity more clearly, I reproduce here one of the season's records of a set of plants that for a long time ceased producing, but at the close of the season carried a considerable quantity of small immature fruits.

VARIETY LIVINGSTON'S BEAUTY.

Date of Harvest.	No. fruits	Weight lbs and tenths.	No. rotted	Weight.
July 17	5	1.2	3	.6
July 21	4	.8		
July 25	11	2.9	6	1.3
July 28	20	6.8	7	1.8
July 31	33	9.4	10	2.3
Aug. 4	55	18.0	14	4.3
Aug. 7	41	14.4	6	1.6
Aug. 11	198	51.3	14	3.2
Aug. 14	93	21.2	15	2.4
Aug. 17	69	8.1	11	1.8
Aug. 21	14	1.9	4	.6
Aug. 25	1	.2		
Aug. 28	5	.6		
Sep 1	10	1.6	2	.3
Sep, 4	10	1.7		
Sep 8	2	.3		
Sep. 11	6	.6		
Sep 18	2	.2		

From the record given above it is evident that the yield decreased rapidly from Aug. 11th to Aug. 25th when a single fruit was gathered from the 10 plants. Instead of a decreased product at this period the plants should have been making their greatest yield. From Aug. 25th on there is a slight restoration, but that was only temporary. From my knowledge of the general behavior of tomato plants, I am convinced that in this section the tomato crop was reduced fully 20% by the excessive rains.

These results were general in this vicinity, for special inquiry was made of all market gardeners who dealt in Morgantown and it was learned that they had had the same experience.

This peculiar behavior seems to have been the result of the extraordinary climatic conditions existing during the growing season. About the time the young plants were setting the field, and for some time thereafter, the precipitation was normal or slightly below; later it began to rain, and kept it up from day to day until the records for July show a rainfall never before chronicled in this section of West Virginia. It is a well known fact that heavy rains at blooming time will destroy the fruit crop of the season. Apples, pears and plums all suffer from this cause, but never before has a like result come under my observation with one of the garden vegetables.